LOOKOUT LAND
PIRATES' BAY
LITTLE LOOKOUTS' TREE HOUSE
LOOKOUT POINT
FAIRMEADOW
SHIPWRECK COVE
N
NE
E
SE
S
SW
W
NW

D1032139

Published by Modern Publishing,
a Division of Unisystems, Inc.

Copyright ©1987 Modern Publishing and Carnival Press, Inc.

®Honey Bear Books is a trademark owned by Honey Bear Productions, Inc., and is registered in the U.S. Patent and Trademark Office.

"Little Lookouts,"™ and the characters in this book, are licensed trademarks of Carnival Press, Inc.

No part of this book may be reproduced or copied without written permission from the publisher.

All Rights Reserved.

Printed in Singapore.

The Little Lookouts™
Discover the Alphabet

Written by Cliff Ellwood
Illustrated by Nathan Y. Jarvis and George F. Martin

Modern Publishing
A Division of Unisystems, Inc.
New York, New York 10022

John LaFeet knocked loudly on the Little Lookouts' treehouse door.

"I just found a treasure map under a rock," explained the nasty pirate. "Can we use your airplane and train to find the treasure?"

Christopher, Joan, Lewis, Clark, Amelia, and Cortez thought this would be a great adventure!

"This treasure map follows the alphabet!" said Christopher. "And letter **A** is first."

"**A** is for **A**pple Valley," said Joan, "the place where we begin our treasure hunt."

A a

So the Lookouts and John LaFeet rushed to **A**pple Valley. They found other things there that began with the letter **A**: **a**rrow, **a**nchor, **a**nt, and **a**lligator.

"The map says letter **B** is next," exclaimed Lewis. "**B** is for the **B**erry **B**ushes — let's go!"

B b

At the **B**erry **B**ushes, they all found the Little Lookouts' airplane. There were three big **b**alloons on the airplane to help it fly! The Lookouts also found a **b**asket, a **b**one, and a **b**all.

Amelia flew everyone in her Little Lookouts' airplane. "Letter **C** is next," she said. "The treasure map says we have to go to **C**ookie **C**astle. Yummy!"

At the **c**astle, Amelia ate too many **c**ookies and **c**andy **c**anes.

Lewis and Clark liked the **c**ake, the **c**otton **c**andy, and the **c**ups of hot **c**ocoa.

"Don't eat too many sweets," warned Joan.

"Letter **D** is for **D**aisy Field!" squawked Cortez.

The Little Lookouts and John LaFeet flew over **D**aisy Field.

"Look," shouted Cortez. "I see a **d**ragon eating **d**oughnuts with a **d**uck and a **d**onkey — all in **D**aisy Field!"

"Hurry, hurry— what letter comes next?" asked John.

"The next letter is **E**," said Clark, holding the treasure map. "And **E** is for **E**lephant Village!"

Amelia flew the Lookouts to **E**lephant Village. “Hello, **e**lephants!” called Amelia. “I see you have lots of **e**ggs, **e**ngines, **e**meralds, and **e**nvelopes today.”

"We've got to hike on foot to the next spot on the map," laughed Joan. "I'm glad that **F** is for **F**unny **F**orest!"

They watched a **f**ox eating **f**udge by a **f**ountain. There's always something funny happening in **F**unny **F**orest!

“Stay close to me, everybody,” warned Christopher. “The treasure map says we have to go to letter **G** next, and **G** is for **G**hostville!”

G g

“**G**olly!” whispered Lewis. “I see a **g**host playing a **g**uitar, a **g**host eating a **g**rapefruit, a **g**host wearing **g**loves, and a **g**host with a **g**ift.”

“Let’s get out of here!” shrieked John LaFeet.

"I'm glad we're out of those spooky woods," gasped Lewis. "Next are the letters **H** and **I**, and they stand for **H**igh **H**ill and **I**nk Lake."

I i

They found **h**orses eating **h**otdogs on **H**igh **H**ill and **i**guanas playing **i**nstruments near **I**nk Lake.

"I think their **h**ats are silly," said Amelia, "but I like the music from their **i**nstruments."

J j

“Oh, I think I’m going to love the next stop on the treasure map,” drooled Amelia. “Next are letters **J** and **K**, and they stand for the **J**ellybean **K**itchen!”

Amelia ran all the way to the Lookout Land **J**ellybean **K**itchen.

K k

“Look at all the **j**ellybeans in **j**ars and **k**ettles,” said Joan.

The Lookouts also saw a **k**itten flying a **k**ite with a **k**ey on it!

"Follow me," ordered Amelia. "The next stop on the map is just down the road. The letters **L** and **M** stand for **L**ollipop **M**anor, home of the **L**ollipop **M**an!"

They found the **L**ollipop **M**an making **l**ollipops. "Welcome to my kitchen," said the **L**ollipop **M**an. "I'm putting lots of **l**emons and **l**imes into my **l**ollipops. My **m**onkey friend can give you some **m**ilk and **m**uffins while you're waiting for the **l**ollipops to cook."

"Next are letters **N** and **O**," said Cortez. "They stand for the **N**eighborhood of **N**ests by the **o**cean."

"There are big **n**ests by the **o**cean," said Lewis. "And a friendly **o**ctopus swims there all the time!"

The Lookouts found the **n**ests, a **n**ewspaper, a **n**ecklace, some **o**lives, and the friendly **o**ctopus in the **o**cean.

"Next stop," said Clark, "is **P** and **Q** — the **P**alace of **Q**uilts!"

John and the Lookouts hiked into the Sleepy Mountains and finally reached the **P**alace of **Q**uilts.

Q q

“Good morning, **Q**ueen of **Q**uilts,” said Joan, bowing. “Your **p**alace of **p**illows and **p**ajamas and **q**uilts is on our treasure map.”

But it was no use — the **q**ueen was asleep at her **p**iano!

“We’ll have fun at our next stop,” said Joan, reading the treasure map. “The next letter is **R**, and **R** is for the **R**obot Factory!”

Even John LaFeet had a good time with the **r**obots. They played on **r**oller skates, **r**ocked on a **r**ocking horse, played **r**ecords, and helped build a **r**ocket!

Christopher studied the treasure map carefully. “Next is letter **S**, and **S** is for the **S**uper **S**andbox!”

The Little Lookouts played in the **S**uper **S**andbox. Lewis and Clark found a **s**ailboat and a **s**hovel. Joan dug holes with a **s**poon, and John built a pirate **s**tatue. Amelia ate a **s**andwich.

The next place on the treasure map was the **T**rain **T**racks, because **T** is for **t**rain.

"All aboard," said Clark. "My Little Lookouts' **t**rain is filled with **t**oy **t**rucks, **t**oy **t**eapots, **t**oy **t**rumpets, and **t**oy **t**ops!"

T t

"This **t**rain can **t**ake us **t**o **t**he **t**reasure," said Lewis, looking a**t** **t**he **t**reasure map.

U u

As the Little Lookouts and John LaFeet took the train ride to the treasure, they had to roll past letters **U** and **V**. They stood for the **U**mbrella Trees and **V**alentine **V**olcano.

V v

"Everybody put up your **u**mbrellas," ordered Amelia. "We'll need them when we ride past **V**alentine **V**olcano!"

Valentine hearts poured out of the **v**olcano and bounced off the Little Lookouts' **u**mbrellas.

"We're almost there," squawked Cortez. "I see **W** and **X** right now! **W** is for **W**ishing **W**aterfall and **X** is for **X** marks the spot— and our treasure."

The Lookouts stopped by the **w**aterfall and a large **w**indmill. They found a **w**atermelon patch, and right in the middle was a big **X** to mark where the treasure was.

"I can hardly wait to dig up the treasure!" said John LaFeet. "I know this will be the best treasure I ever found!"

Y y

John dug and dug, and finally his shovel struck the lid of a treasure chest. Thud!

He hauled up the chest and slowly opened its lid, and what do you think the treasure was?

Z z

It was **y**o-**y**os and lots of **z**ippers!

The Little Lookouts just laughed and laughed at the funny treasure.

Aa Bb Cc Dd Ee Ff Gg

Oo Pp Qq Rr Ss Tt Uu

The Little Lookouts had fun on their alphabet treasure hunt. They took John LaFeet and his yo-yos and zippers back to their train. Choo-choo, choo-choo!

Hh Ii Jj Kk Ll Mm Nn

Vv Ww Xx Yy Zz

Can you name all the letters of the alphabet?

OCEAN
WITCH WAY FOREST
BALONE
SANDY
WITCH
CASTL.
FORGET-ME-NOT POND
Very Cranberry Canal
OCEAN